THE
Homecoming

For M - who shared the journey with me

THE Homecoming
Randolph O'Hara

Orchid Press

Published by
ORCHID PRESS
P. O. Box 19,
Yutthitham Post Office,
Bangkok, Thailand
www.orchidbooks.com

Designed by
Hon Design & Associates

Copyright © Randolph O'Hara, 2005

Protected by copyright under the terms of the International Copyright Union:
all rights reserved. No part of this publication may be reproduced in any form or
by any means, electronic or mechanical, including photocopying, recording,
or by any information storage or retrieval system
without prior permission in writing from the Publisher.

Printed in Thailand
ISBN 974-524-079-6

FSMDL

Contents

Chapter One ~ The Journey Home   3

Chapter Two ~ Yangon   9

Chapter Three ~ The Old Church   17

Chapter Four ~ Remembrance   23

Chapter Five ~ The Shwedagon   31

Chapter Six ~ Bagan   37

Chapter Seven ~ Mandalay   45

Chapter Eight ~ Largest Book in the World   53

Chapter Nine ~ The Shan States   61

Chapter Ten ~ Yangon Again   67

Conclusion ~ The Golden Land   73

A Brief Note by Way of Introduction

Since writing Fragments from the Past he had thought seriously off and on about visiting Burma and tried, initially, to go with a group, feeling that there was safety in numbers. However, there were no group tours to be found, and as his other possible overseas visit fell through because of cost, he decided to undertake the visit, with some misgivings as a FIT (Foreign Individual Traveller).

Before leaving he noted down all critical telephone numbers, including those of his Embassy and alternative airlines which flew in and out of the country more frequently than the national carrier. His apprehension only eased when he checked into his hotel in the capital. But actually there was no real need for all this concern, as the following account shows.

Chapter One ~ The Journey Home

He sat gazing out of the window at the grey church spire in the distance, which towered above the other buildings on Boyoke Aung San street, named after the country's most revered martyr. The early morning sun glinted over the buildings, and on closer inspection he was surprised to discover that the spire was clad in bamboo scaffolding. Despite the poverty, the church was being maintained, but then this was typical of the country.

On the surface, all seemed the same as he remembered it; yet not the same. The very site on which his hotel stood had in the past housed the well-known Continental restaurant, which was the venue for the annual Good Friday tea treat for the church choir, as well as a number of cinemas. He remembered queuing at the hole-in-the-wall box office in the street adjacent to the hotel to make sure that he got his ticket for the latest cinema offering. Nearer the time of the opening of the box office, the orderly queue could turn into a *melee* and this was when friends were particularly useful, as they helped to keep others at bay. Some of these friends were now dead, having died in exile; others might just as well have been dead because they were lost with the passage of time, and he had no knowledge of their whereabouts.

He looked forward to visiting the church, yet a part of him was afraid of what he might encounter. This sense of foreboding, or nervousness, had been with him ever since he finalized the arrangements to visit the old country and only lessened in the hotel lobby, which seemed like the lobby of any four star international hotel. But was it? The sliced imported meat and cheese in pressurized cellophane packets were incongruous additions to the hotel's small cake shop in the lobby and reminded him of his childhood days when cheese—and it was processed cheese in tins—was an occasional luxury. The dead mosquitoes on the parapet floor were also not typical of hotel coffee shops elsewhere.

His thoughts strayed further to his journey into the country. Sometime before the small plane landed he looked out of the window and was surprised that all the land as far as his eyes could see was under cultivation, presumably rice cultivation, for which the country had been famous. Yet if there was cultivation on this scale why was the country given least developed nation status by the United Nations? Something must be wrong somewhere, and he assumed it was the usual story of mis-management and bad government, if not outright corruption.

He had been told that the airport terminal had not been redeveloped, but could not remember what it looked like. He had two recollections of the airport, neither of them about the physical make-up of the building. His first recollection was of a dull overcast grey day when the most important person in his life at the time was leaving the country. He watched at a distance from the hired bus with a deepening sense of sadness as others said their 'good-byes', but could not bring himself to do the same. On returning to the city he had somehow managed to meet up with his cousin and they went to see the latest Danny Kaye offering of Hans Christian Andersen at a now defunct cinema, adjacent to where his present hotel stood. But the film, tinged with sadness, had failed to cheer him up. His other recollection was one of excitement as after prolonged days of delay he left on his first overseas trip. He did not have any luggage to speak of, but was carrying six flexible bamboo canes at the request of his host. He must have made an odd sight: a fresh faced teenager with six canes, and probably aroused all kinds of latent stirrings amongst masochists in the crowd.

On de-planing, the word 'International' at the airport building caught his attention. The word would have been laughable, if it wasn't sad, because apart from two airlines from neighbouring countries, the only international flights were those of the country's national carrier, and even then from only one or two nearby destinations and about twice a week at that. The terminal was a bare rectangular building with a high ceiling, but badly lit, and there was the usual throng of bureaucrats, particularly at the customs counter. One noted down rather desultorily the fact that he possessed a ring and a gold chain around his neck, but otherwise they showed no interest in him. On leaving the terminal building he was surprised at the absence of the normal bustle that one usually encountered, but then remembered that the country was not a favourite destination with tourists, and the plane on which he had traveled had no more than a handful of visitors. However, the soft sunshine that cast long shadows and the smell of sweet flowers mingled with that of earth got to him, and it was like he had never been away. As the car from the airport traversed the wide roads of the suburbs, he noticed that despite it being the dry season, vegetation flourished everywhere, and in the middle of major road intersections there were elaborate gardening arrangements in the form of stupas.

From the window of the car he searched in vain for the old university buildings, and particularly the university's minor staff quarters that had been his home for a while, but there was no trace of them, except for the grey convocation building in the distance. Where had the buildings gone?

Chapter Two ~ Yangon

His itinerary called for a tour of the city's main attractions the next day. Remembering the proximity of the attractions, he had agreed that part of the tour could be on foot, because he wanted to get a better feel of the city as it was today. Despite this arrangement, he could not wait and decided to walk around the block before dinner.

The narrow, uneven pavements were packed solid with itinerant sellers and food vendors, leaving only a small lane for pedestrians. Goods were simply displayed on plastic sheets and consisted of plastic knick-knacks, men's shirts in plastic bags with fake designer labels, sports shoes and local slippers. Some of the goods were obviously obtained from the thriving 'black market'. As for the food vendors, he noticed Indian sweet meats and bread, cauldrons of the broth of the national dish *Mohinga* and what appeared to be the innards of pigs. People squatted on small stools and ate with relish facing the food vendors, as there were no tables or chairs.

Lighting was uniformly poor, and those shops that were slightly brighter had their own small generators placed on the pavement, outside of their shops. Despite the dimness, children played merrily, whilst he noticed two men absorbed in a game of chess. He walked along what he thought was a portion of the street name after the first British commissioner of the city, but was puzzled that in the place where there should have been an iron-cast railway bridge with steps there stood a road bridge. Had he got it wrong? Apparently not, because he was told that the military had built a road over the bridge about ten years ago.

Walking the streets, his thoughts strayed to the uncles and father that he had left behind many years ago. Having left them, it seemed somehow strange that they were not here when he had returned. He knew, of course, that this was wishful thinking on his part because if they had been alive they would have been in their centenary years. Yet it somehow didn't seem the same without them. His dear, talented, hard-working and eternally optimistic father, in particular. His father could not have had an easy life. He recalled how one day, when searching for something, he came across a letter written to his father by his mother soon after she had left them. He knew he should not read it, and didn't read all of it, but the words 'I love somebody else...you were always a gentleman' sprang out from the hand-written page, and struck a chord with him so much so that he could still remember the words today. How much harder it must have been for his father who had kept the letter all those years, as some kind of tenuous link with the past.

There appeared to be a lot more cars on the road, especially white coloured taxis, which he learnt later were discards from elsewhere. But who were taking these taxis in this poverty stricken country? Apparently, lots of people, because the taxis were in great demand. Some of the thoroughfares were one way, and Sule Pagoda road, one of the main transport arteries through the city had high wire mesh dividers. However, the bus service was as rudimentary as he remembered. The buses were hard seat affairs, and appeared to be converted lorries with a low roof, so low that one could hardly see the faces of the sitting passengers. A feature of the bus service, which he had forgotten, was the use of driver's helpers on the rear wooden platform. It was their job to keep other vehicles at bay or to guide the driver in highly congested situations. At one particular bus stop that he passed, there appeared to be no discernible order, and as soon as the bus arrived, the waiting passengers threw their bags through the windows on to the seats, before getting on.

Later, he noticed from his hotel room window that the railway station with its stupa-like pinnacles continued to dominate the cityscape of that area. The station held many memories for him, as it used to be his morning starting point to the soft drinks factory in the suburbs where he worked for a time as a bottle-washer. It was also where he stayed during windy, rainy days in his childhood as his father had an absolute phobia about storms and insisted at the slightest indication of an impending storm that the family take shelter at the railway station. In the evenings, the platforms of the station were filled with sleeping passengers awaiting their late night or early morning trains. On one occasion, when he was much older, he was told that a man and a woman were discovered sleeping inside the man's *longyi*—a sarong-type garment worn by both men and women—with the intention no doubt of doing what comes naturally. He never did discover whether or not they were successful.

Dinner that evening, which wasn't very good, was of the ubiquitous buffet type, and consisted mainly of rice and noodle dishes. The restaurant took the shape of a boat, built in the local style but of stone, and was therefore permanently moored at one end of what used to be known as the Royal Lakes. Included with the dinner were performances of traditional puppets and dancing which partly made up for the poor food. The dancers wore richly coloured tight fitting garments, and the dancing consisted for the most part of stylized hand and leg movements.

The next morning he was asked by his guide: "Are you sure you want to walk for part of the tour?" and his answer was an emphatic "Yes". The first attraction was the well-known Sule Pagoda in the city. Whilst much smaller than its bigger and better-known sister in the outskirts, it had its own unique charm, being well proportioned and beautifully gilded in gold. A unique feature of this pagoda was that it stood right in the middle of a busy cross-roads. Getting into or out of the pagoda was a hazardous affair in the absence of traffic lights and zebra crossings, and was probably one of the reasons why it did not get many visitors. He certainly had not been inside it and had no intention of doing so on this occasion. He noticed a small mosque on one side of the pagoda, but there was no sign of Shamies, the small well-known bakery-cum-teashop that used to serve traditional afternoon English tea. The City Hall built in the local style continued to dominate the square near The Sule Pagoda, and on inquiring whether it was used for receptions, he was told 'No, it was the seat of civic government'. Yet he could distinctly recall the wedding reception of his older cousin in that building. A reception for which he had taken great pains, as he had spent an inordinate amount of time polishing his shoes. Apart from the usual speeches and food, it was traditional at wedding receptions for the bride and groom to lead the dance. However, the locals had a much more graphic name for these Western-style dances and called them *Puthabin*, which literally means 'rubbing dance'.

The famous department store at which his well-off uncle used to shop had been turned into government offices and the beautiful red stucco brick High Court building had its gates closed. He remembered being able to walk freely through it and feel the cool breezes in the high-ceilinged corridors as he went to collect his massage fees from one of the neighbours he used to massage and who worked in a ground floor office of the building as a minor clerk.

"The City has buildings of many architectural styles" said the guide. "Look at that building" he said, pointing to a fine colonnaded building. "It is in the English style". He looked more closely and then remembered that his well-off uncle used to work in that building. It now housed the Department of Inland Waterways. Pointing to a building with a tower, the guide said: "That is in a Spanish style". It could, equally, have been Japanese but he didn't say so. "And this is in a Portuguese style". Portuguese? He then remembered reading about Portuguese adventurers and freebooters who had come to the country out of Goa in the 16th and 17th centuries. Two of his best friends during his teen years were brothers with the surname 'Da Silva', descendants of Portuguese forebears who had settled in the country. One of the brothers was now long dead, having died as a teenager of a hole in his heart. Whilst most of the Portuguese were content to offer their skills in musketry to the warring factions, one in particular, Felipe de Brito, was to leave his mark on the history of the country. Although nominally aligned with the forces in the southwest of the country, de Brito had ambitions of his own, and from his stronghold across the river, in what was then known as Syriam, he exercised a stranglehold over foreign trade, forcing the ships to pass through Syriam. Despite having married a daughter of the Viceroy of Goa, help from Goa was not forthcoming when his stronghold was attacked by a numerically far superior force of the rising local monarch. Felipe de Brito's systematic plundering of religious shrines was much resented by the local populace, and on defeat he was treated as a common criminal and impaled. It took him two agonizing days to die.

Chapter Three~The Old Church

He went in search of the old pier, which, during his youth, was the departure point for those leaving the country by ship. He had seen off two lots of cousins there who left for England, as well as a friend going in the opposite direction to Borneo. With the rising tide of nationalism in the fifties, many people were in fact leaving the country.

The old pier was still there, but barricaded. He doubted if there were many emigrants travelling by ship today. The adjacent, single storeyed pier at which ferries crossing the river docked was, surprisingly, in immaculate condition, as was the small garden in front of it. When the ferry docked, passengers poured out, but in an orderly and leisurely fashion, typical of the people. However, the old Strand hotel across the road was all pretension with bamboo cane chairs and hardly a guest in sight. He had originally thought of having either afternoon tea or dinner there, but now thought better of it. The Strand, too, held memories for him. Not least amongst these was of a friend who used to work there and who helped him with some money to 'leave' the country. Sadly, he cannot now remember the name of this friend. He does, however, remember that it was this friend's father who had prepared his own grandfather's body for burial, by trimming his moustache, cutting his nails, combing his hair and putting him in his best clothes.

The street adjacent to the Strand could have been a cul-de-sac in London's Chelsea district, and housed at the corner the pristine white Australian Embassy. There was a local soldier on guard, and photography was prohibited. He knew that the British Embassy was further along the road, and that it now housed a reading room in place of a British Council, but he decided against venturing further. The old British Council premises, at which he used to spend many an hour browsing amongst its books or watching documentaries on different aspects of British life, now looked rather shabby and neglected. Walking away from the Strand he noted with some surprise the dark sludge that had been taken from the open drain and left to fester on the pavement. The country was still full of contradictions.

In the afternoon he visited the famous Bogyoke market, known previously as Scott market, the destination for all visitors to the country. The market was chock-a-block with stalls, but bright and relatively cool considering the time of day. The stalls had some of their goods in small glass-fronted display cabinets, with the rest stacked high behind the raised platforms on which stall owners sat. There was no haggling, and bargaining was done gently. If a particular stall didn't have what one was looking for, its owner was quite prepared to recommend some other stall. Yet, he had been warned, particularly in the matter of gems, that there were many fakes. Not that he had any intention of buying gems. Having obtained a fine lacquer box of horse hair that he had been seeking, he was impatient to visit his old Cathedral church, which was adjacent to the market.

The watchman at the gate kindly let him into the church grounds so that he could take some photographs. On closer inspection, what had appeared to be red bricks were white painted outlines on a red background. There were real bricks in the structure of the building, but they were now so worn they didn't stand out. The grounds were not too well kept, and a small building adjacent to the choir's entrance at the rear of the church appeared to have been added. The adjacent girl's boarding school was still there, and on inquiring, he was told that it was still a girl's school. However, the fence between the church grounds and the school's grounds was higher than he remembered and was now full of creepers, obscuring the school. He remembered how the girls attending Sunday evensong used to crocodile gracefully with white veils over their heads. Sunday evensongs were a bittersweet time for him, for they marked the end of the weekend and the beginning of a new week which held nothing for him, except to loaf, as he did not attend school like his friends. It was also the time when he looked forward to his cold dinner of some kind of curry and rice, eaten on the floor by the light of a kerosene lamp, also placed on the floor, at the back of his house on stilts that served as a kitchen.

The caretaker or verger, he wasn't sure which, kindly let him into the church from the vestry. The interior of the church was much as he remembered it. There were the choir stalls where he had been head chorister and organ boy. But the lovely electronic organ was no more, and had been replaced by a much smaller one, which no longer faced the opposite choir stalls but the congregation. The altar was as high as ever below the lovely stained glass windows, and no attempt had been made to fiddle with this established order, as was the case with some churches in more developed countries. One of the arguments used for moving the altar closer to the congregation and putting the choir stalls at the back of the altar is apparently to bring the services closer to the people. He then thought to himself that in a poor country you needed no gimmicks to bring the people to God. With these reflections, he walked around one of the side chapels. He remembered hearing how his well-off uncle used to lay the law down at church council meetings, and how he had advanced his own *jejune* argument 'that if God created the universe, then who created God' to the priest taking his confirmation class in that very same chapel. Looking around he was pleasantly surprised to see the insignia of the various British army units who had served in the country still on the wall, and his eyes caught the word 'The Howards'. He then recalled how the Cathedral had been the venue for the annual Remembrance Day service. How his young heart used to swell with pride on seeing the representatives from the various embassies, especially the attachés of the armed services with their swords and rows of medals on their chests. He can distinctly remember the sonorous voice of the chaplain reading the well-known words:

> *And they shall not grow old,*
> *As we that are left grow old.*
> *Age shall not weary them...*

These were, of course, words of consolation, because who in their right mind would not prefer to grow old gracefully instead of being cut down in the flower of youth. He could still hear distinctly in the ears of his memory the chaplain's voice bringing the verse to its rather sad ending; with words that went something like:

> *And with the setting of the sun,*
> *We shall remember them,*
> *We shall remember them.*

Chapter Four~Remembrance

He had arranged before arriving in the country for a car to be made available so that he could visit places of his choosing. One of the places that he had planned to visit was the street on which his old house on stilts had stood. The name of the street had, of course, been changed, but taking his bearings from the main railway station, he could easily find his way and direct the guide and driver.

St. Anthony's Church and the adjacent school were as he remembered them, but seemed to have only recently been repainted. He remembered being invited to breakfast one Sunday at the priests' quarters behind the church, and at being pleasantly surprised by the spread of food. The priests obviously did well for themselves.

The stadium, which occupied a large area opposite St.Anthony's Church, was now encrusted with various work-shops, and there was a small mosque as well. Was it always there? He could not remember. He recalled watching boxing as well as football and hockey matches at the stadium, and how his uncle used to cry animatedly "sticks, sticks" at a hockey match between two school teams. The two-storeyed buildings that served as railway quarters were now no more; gone, too, were the taller buildings near the market where his aunt and her family used to live before emigrating, but the self-contained larger house nearer the railway station was still there. He remembered playing with a younger boy at this house at a make-believe tent with biscuits and tea, but could not now remember either the boy's name or the name of the family.

Further on, he noted with a tinge of sadness that all the houses, including his old house on stilts, had been demolished, but amongst the more substantial brick buildings that now stood in their place his eye caught a smaller wood and brick structure with a small gate in front. Was that the grand house that the neighbour had built? A seller of lottery tickets, it had been rumoured that he won the lottery, so could build the house. Wherever his sudden wealth came from, to celebrate the completion of the house, he had monks in for a prayer session and invited all the neighbours, serving the most delicious chicken *biryani* at the celebrations. However, the dish may not have been that extraordinary, and may only have been embedded in his memory by the plain fare he had everyday.

In fact, he could not rationalize with himself why he had been eager to seek out the old house on stilts. It held few good memories for him. He recalled that they had moved to the house or rather one quarter of it, from their lovely old house in Insein on the outskirts of the city, which was his first home on returning to the country after the war. He had quite a few friends then, who lived in similar houses, and it was perhaps the happiest time of his childhood.

He recalled how they, boys and girls, used to congregate to play in the afternoons, and how his own house was always full of people, from his paternal grandfather to his uncle who stayed with them. One evening, a portion of the floor close to where his grandfather used to sit gave way and left a huge gaping hole in the floor. They all said how fortunate it was that his grandfather wasn't sitting in the usual place when this happened. He used to play below the house as there was a large open space there, the house actually starting from one floor up, and remembered chasing a hen with his cousin in the hope that the hen could be persuaded to lay an egg. The poor hen after a great deal of running to and fro did lay an egg in her fright. He and his cousin then had to decide where to hide the egg, and came up with the bright idea of putting the egg into the pocket of his father's jacket that had hung close to the front door without being used for some time. Having placed the egg in the jacket pocket, they were dismayed when his father took down the jacket and put it on, smashing the egg in the process. Their dismay was only matched by the surprise on his father's face.

He recalled another occasion when he and his cousin thought of themselves as great thespians and decided to put on a play which they had made up. They announced the forthcoming play to all their friends and asked them to bring a small coin for admission. The friends duly turned up and when they counted the coins they found that they had an odd number. This meant that one of them would get more than the other, which would never do. So one little boy was persuaded to return home to get another coin. However, this aroused the suspicion of his mother who decided to come and investigate. The two aspiring thespians saw her and the boy from a distance and decided the best course of action would be to do a quick bunk, and the planned performance broke up in disarray.

In contrast, the house on stilts was for the most part a miserable existence, filled with nothing but chores and occasional beatings. He was also the only one in the family to be given a nickname. He was called 'Ah Pui', meaning 'bulging eyes' in the native language. Well, he had big eyes, but he didn't think they bulged. The ironic thing is one of them is now made of glass. On one occasion when playing by the roadside with his young siblings in tow, a jeep drove past and on looking up he caught the eyes of some of his erstwhile friends from Insein. They too were surprised to see him, and must have wondered what he was doing by the side of the road far away from his old house. Sanitation in the whole street was dreadful. The toilets were some distance from the house, and consisted of a small hut divided into two raised platforms, with buckets below. He dreaded having to visit the toilets at night because there was no light and he imagined all kinds of mysterious creatures lurking in the swaying banana plants. The country had no 'perfumed ladies of the night', and the toilets were cleaned by men during the daytime. The cleaning did not take place that often and the only reason why the buckets did not overflow was because the stray, hungry dogs ate the excrement, or some of it, with the rest festering into maggots. Little wonder then that the World Health Organization used to visit frequently to show hygiene documentaries on a make-shift screen by the roadside.

Suffering from malnutrition and with poor hygiene it was only the strength of youth that prevented him from getting seriously ill. He did, however, catch a bug one year and had never felt so cold in his life, despite the heat and sunshine. His step-mother was too preoccupied with her own affairs to notice, whilst his dear father was far too busy trying to earn a living. He remembered waiting for his father at the YMCA, feeling miserably cold and watching others play table tennis to pass the time. He knew his father used the YMCA as a refreshment stop between home visits to give private tuition. The refreshment consisted for the most part of tea sweetened with condensed milk, as his father had lost all of his teeth many years earlier and could not easily eat solid food. On seeing him, his father professed no surprise, and after offering him a cup of tea to warm him up, was on his way again. He usually went to each pupil's house on foot as he was a fast walker. Whatever it was that had invaded his body, it seems to have stayed with him and lies dormant except each spring when it would manifest itself and he could feel unwell. Some years are worse than others.

27

More often than not, there was barely enough to eat. In order to supplement their home fare, he and the neighbourhood boys attempted to catch fish in the large open water catchment that flowed near their homes. They had no fishing rods, but relied on their hands as the water was quite shallow. Once he got something long and slippery which escaped his clutches. They thought it might have been an eel, but it could equally have been a water snake. The main hazard with fishing this way was the leeches. They would latch onto his legs, sucking his blood, and there was no way of getting them off, except by burning them. They would then leave spoor marks on his calves.

On another occasion they decided to hunt for flying birds with their catapults. He managed to kill a crow, probably by luck, and they plucked the bird where it fell, lit a small fire and roasted it. Even in their hunger, it tasted horrible: sour, stringy and tough.

However, it was not just him that was hungry. From the zoo nearby he used to hear the lion roar at night. It is an awesome sound, and people said that the lion roared because it was hungry, as they dare not feed it to its full, lest the lion gets strong and jumps over the long iron bars in the open air part of the its cage. The roaring may, of course, have been due to frustration. On inquiring from his driver who lived near the zoo, he was told that the lion no longer roars at night. This may be because the lion's appetite had slowed, like his, with age, or that it was resigned to its fate.

However, he liked to think that the real reason why it no longer roared was because it was now better fed.

He remembered that part of his routine was to walk over the railway bridge and loaf around the town, taking in the YMCA and the British Council library. In the afternoons, he would make the return journey by the same route. One afternoon, he met the daughter of a family that his father used to know. They lived in one of the nice railway houses, so the girl and he walked over the bridge together. She was a well-meaning girl, but on noticing that his trousers were torn in the seat, she said, "Why don't you wear something better?" He felt rather embarrassed by the question to which he had no answer. Today, of course, it is fashionable to wear jeans that have been deliberately slashed in the front and at the back, and if the jeans carry the name of a well-known designer, the wealthy pay a fortune for the privilege of doing so.

Chapter Five ~ The Shwedagon

An essential sight for all visitors to the country is, of course, the Shwedagon Pagoda. He had visited the pagoda once before, many years ago, but had no particular memories of it. Translated literally, the name of the pagoda means gold dagon, dagon being the old name for the capital before the British named it Rangoon. Today the capital is called Yangon, which sounds rather like a local translation of Rangoon, but is probably not.

The origins of the Shwedagon is lost in mythology, but it probably started as a much smaller structure which was periodically rebuilt, getting larger with each rebuilding. The pagoda is visible from most parts of the city, but is at its most beautiful at dawn or sunset.

Approaching closer to the pagoda he saw a long series of covered steps and thought that he had a long climb ahead of him. However, visitors from elsewhere, especially foreign visitors, are shunted to a separate entrance and from there are taken to the second, main level, by lift. Removal of shoes and even socks are obligatory before entering any structure of the pagoda complex, and he left his in the van.

Despite all the pictures that have been taken and all the written descriptions of the pagoda, none can do it justice, and he was overawed by the magnificence of the whole complex, and by the way people went about their business making offerings and meditating. Despite the crowds there was no noise or clamour, and all was serene and inspiring.

The pagoda, which is reputed to house a number of hairs of the Buddha, is a complex of structures, rather than a single structure. The main structure or stupa, in the shape of an inverted cone, rises over three hundred feet from the ground. Surrounding it on all sides are smaller structures devoted to different days of the week and different subjects, and he noticed one statue of the Buddha holding an infant. Couples seeking a son come before this statue to ask for help. Help is sought by praying before the statue, *shiko*-ing before it (that is genuflecting with the feet tucked behind and the head touching the floor), by making offerings of fruit and garlands of flowers, and by pouring water gently over it, from the shallow wells near the statues. People pay homage before the statue for a particular day of the week either because it happens to be the day of their visit, or more importantly, because they were born on that particular day. Given the date and year of birth, the locals can not only calculate the day of the week on which a person was born, but also can determine whether the person is hot tempered, short tempered or even tempered. Of course, no one wishes to be categorized as either a short or hot tempered person.

Walking around the various statues, the guide said, "That is the statue for Wednesday; that is also for

Wednesday". So he asked how it was that Wednesday had two different statues, and was told that unlike other days of the week, Wednesday is divided into two: morning and afternoon, but he never discovered why it was so.

In front of the statues is a relatively wide piazza made of large cool tiles, which surrounds the whole structure. Behind it are other structures which are covered but open on all sides, and which hold either statues, scriptures or bells. Some are intended mainly for shelter from the elements. They are made of concrete or wood, and in some cases are inlaid with innumerable small mirrors that glittered and sparkled as the light caught them. Monks were conspicuous by their absence, because the pagoda is not a monastery, and he only noticed a few young novices sitting meekly in one of the structures whilst their photographs were taken. Despite a clear but simple gesture that the photographer should donate something to their lacquer bowls, their pleas was boorishly ignored by the foreign, Western visitors, who could well afford to make a small donation.

One of the most significant ways to obtain blessing is to coat the statues with small and very thin pieces of real gold foil. A small packet was accordingly purchased and the gold applied to a statue, but with some difficulty as there is a technique to it. Not applied properly, the gold foil simply coils back on itself and disintegrates. He became more adept after a few tries, but was better at placing the foil on the statue's legs rather than face, which he could not reach properly. Because of the belief that blessing is obtained from applying gold leaf, the main pagoda and all the subsidiary Buddha statues at the base of the pagoda are coated with tons of pure gold, and this in a poor country.

Later on in the city of Mandalay he saw how the gold foil was made. A very small piece of gold foil was placed between thick sheets of paper and then pounded until it became bigger and gossamer thin. The pounding was an arduous task, and the two men worked in rotation and in a particular rhythm. They were also thin as blades which was not surprising because the pounder was very heavy and he could hardly lift it when he tried.

Although the Shwedagon is the most famous structure in the country, its upkeep is left largely to private donors and he noticed signs showing how much it cost to maintain different features of the pagoda, as well as acknowledgements of donations from Buddhist organizations from different parts of the world.

In his travels he had seen many impressive structures devoted to Buddhism but none, he thought, were as beautiful as the Shwedagon. He was to discover that there were many beautiful golden pagodas and

Buddha images throughout the country, each with its own unique history and features, as well as charm. No wonder then that the country is known as 'The Golden Land'.

Chapter Six~Bagan

The flight to Bagan (or Pagan as it used to be known) was an early one, necessitating a morning call at 4:00 AM in the hotel. Unlike the calm of the international arrivals' hall, the scene at the domestic departure hall could only be described as 'chaotic order'. On the surface, everything appeared to be chaotic with no discernible counters for different flights or orderly queues. Piles of luggage could be seen in different parts of the small hall, which was also packed with passengers and their 'helpers'. Two helpers soon took charge of him, one disappearing with his tickets and another with his luggage. There was simply no use worrying whether the luggage would ever be seen again. In a few minutes one of the helpers appeared with his boarding pass and the other with his luggage tag. Money changed hands, because it was obligatory for the helpers to be paid, and the helpers disappeared to help other passengers.

On entering the small departure hall, which was full of passengers, he noticed that the small flight display board showed flight numbers that bore no relationship to his flight number. After a while, he inquired of a fellow passenger whether he was going to Bagan. He was told 'Yes' and shown a boarding pass, but it was for a different airline. Meanwhile, luggage by the cartload was going through the same departure gates intended for passengers, and shortly afterwards a man with a placard showing a flight number did the rounds of the departure hall, calling out the flight details. Passengers who were absent minded were recognized by the man from the flight stickers that all passengers were encouraged to wear, and urged to proceed through the departure gates. Soon it was his time to board, and he went through the gates to walk to his plane. After the stuffiness of the departure hall, the cool morning breeze and sunshine was exhilarating, and his spirits lifted.

The journey was uneventful and in no time they were descending into Bagan airport. The airport was a delightful small one storeyed building, surrounded by green foliage and large bushes of bougainvillaea. His guide met him in the arrival hall, something that the guide in the capital was not allowed to do, and took charge of collecting his luggage.

The drive to his hotel was smooth and quick despite the fact that there were only two lanes of road, one in each opposite direction, separated by a row of trees and plants. He soon discovered that the reason for the absence of traffic was because there were actually two Bagans: the old archaeological Bagan in which he was travelling; and the new Bagan which was much more recent and where most local people lived. The hotel was of the resort type and the idyllic and modern setting contrasted sharply with the rather bare room and poor lighting. The lighting was so poor that he couldn't really see enough to do anything in the room. On request a few thin plastic hangers were provided for the open wardrobe that had seen better days.

However, these minor inconveniences were soon forgotten as they set off to see the world famous pagodas of Bagan. Actually, not all the structures are pagodas. Some are monasteries and others halls of meditation. The more famous of the structures were suitably spaced, not to impinge upon each other. Their first stop was the Shwezigon Pagoda, which date to about the time that William the Conqueror invaded Britain. Built by King Anawrahta, the founder of the Bagan dynasty, in 1059, it was completed by his son, King Kyanzittha and houses Buddha's collar bone, frontal bone and miraculously duplicated tooth from what is now Sri Lanka. In appearance it looked like a squat and smaller version of the Shwedagon in the capital. King Anawrahta introduced Theravada Buddhism (the earlier and more conservative form of Buddhism that is prevalent throughout South East Asia) into the country and was clever enough to realize that the only way he could convert the inhabitants of the country to Buddhism would be to incorporate traditional worship of the Nat spirits into the scheme of things. It was, therefore, not incongruous to find a smaller hall of Nats within the temple complex. Looking at the hall of Nats he recalled how in his youth he used to watch with curiosity and fear the roadside ceremonies at which men volunteered to have themselves possessed by a

Nat. The traditional animistic religion believed that Nats were capable of causing both harm and good, and he had watched the possessed men in the hope that in their benevolence the spirits possessing the men would hand over some of the men's money to him. Unfortunately this never happened.

As with all temples in the country, there were numerous young monks who were prepared to have their photographs taken in return for a small contribution. One young seated monk, on making eye contact, beckoned to him by gently patting his black lacquer bowl. When he refused to take his photograph the young monk looked crestfallen, but with a resigned look on his face. The expression on the boy's face stirred something within him, so he offered to take his picture, to be rewarded with a big smile for the camera, something that the young monks don't normally do. After making a quick round of a shrine behind the young monk, he noticed that the young monk had gone, and he liked to think that having raised his contribution for the day for the monastery he had left.

Their next stop was the famous Ananda Temple, built by King Kyanzittha in 1090. The temple is of a most unusual structure, consisting of a series of terraces on top of which stood the beehive-shaped spire, capped by a golden stupa. It is built in the shape of a Greek cross and, unlike the Shwezigon, is a cave-like structure with high ceilings. On inquiring about the height of the ceilings, the guide said to him, "In summer it gets so hot here, it is unbearable. We cannot stay at home, so come to the temple to keep cool". However, this was not the reason for the height of the corridors, but it probably took that form in keeping with the four colossal standing golden Buddhas, facing north, south, east and west, that the temple housed.

The history of Bagan is a strange mixture of piety and violence and its annals are filled with the murders of siblings, off-spring and parents which may in part account for the proliferation of religious structures, which were more likely than not built as atonement for these crimes. Most of Bagan was probably destroyed by the inhabitants themselves in an attempt to provide fortifications against the Tartar hordes of Kublai Khan which overran the city.

Lunch was at a delightful open-air restaurant overlooking the Irrawaddy River. A most relaxing environment, even if the food was insipid and the flies were a distraction. In the afternoon, they visited further temples, but that which made the most impression on him was Kyanzittha cave temple with its long dark corridors, embellished with frescoes from the 11th to the 13th centuries. The temple was apparently used by monks to meditate.

Together with others they watched the sunset over the plains from a temple. As the day waned and the sun gradually sank, the colours of the sky changed from rose and gold to lavender and lilac and the various religious structures silhouetted against it grew gradually darker, until they disappeared altogether. Waiting for the sunset, he noticed three mothers with their teenaged daughters. The mothers were as shy as the daughters were vivacious, and despite repeated exhortations to pose for the camera sat demurely as their photographs were taken.

Dinner was at a restaurant with open torch-lit fires, reminiscent of Hawaii. The restaurant was famous for its puppet show. The puppetry is skilled and one reason for this is to be found in the modesty of the people. He recalled that for dramatic performances in Elizabethan England, boys usually played the parts of women. The people of this country were even more modest, and could not bear to see any form of intimacy between people on the stage. So wooden figures were called into play and did what flesh and blood could not do. The Puppet show he saw featured a variety of characters as well as animals, and the crowd scenes were particularly impressive. After the performance, the puppeteers with their puppets made the rounds of the tables to say Mingalaba or 'Hello' to everyone.

Returning to his hotel room, he flipped through the TV to discover that the hotel had limited satellite TV, and surprisingly had Fashion TV. The swimwear and lingerie featured would be considered provocative even by the standards of the outside world, and he wondered what relevance the channel could possibly have to a country where everyone wore the conservative, traditional garb, and more particularly so to the holy city of Bagan. With these thoughts he was soon fast asleep.

Chapter Seven~Mandalay

Early morning Bagan, even more so than in Yangon, is cool and serene. He was told that breakfast was in the garden, which rather non-plussed him because the whole hotel setting was like a garden. After further inquiry at the hotel's reception, he was pointed in the right direction.

The garden was a large open space at the rear of the hotel. It was really a lawn, punctuated by bushes and trees, and lit by dim coloured lanterns. At one end was a large, manned, serving table. He decided to have a native breakfast, but both the *Mohinga* and *Kyaungyinbaung* were not up to scratch, the latter in particular, being cold and without the desiccated coconut or spiced salt. However, the coffee was black, strong and excellent, and two cups of it soon perked him up.

The flight to Mandalay, the city made famous for English readers by Rudyard Kipling, was just half an hour in duration, but the drive from Mandalay airport to the town centre took about an hour. The airport is modern, but bare, and it was the first time he saw a luggage conveyor belt in the country. Unfortunately, the toilets were jammed because of a blocked drain.

His guide read out the itinerary for the first day in the car. The suggested itinerary seemed to reverse the order of the two-day itinerary given to him before his arrival in the country, but was a more logical one. The first stop was Amarapura, the ancient capital, before King Mindon, the second but last King of the country, decided to move his capital to Mandalay. However, the Chinese population decided to stay in Amarapura, which now has a large Chinese community, and on the drive in he noticed a well-kept Chinese temple.

They drove through a village of small, shaded winding streets, and en-route came upon an elephant procession, with the elephants caparisoned in rich red silks and tinkling bells, but the procession was *sans* the famous white elephant, which is the symbol of the Kings of the country. He was told that the capital had a white elephant. Although he did not see it, he did get an embroidered likeness of it.

Amarapura has from time immemorial been famed for its silk, and he bought himself a *longyi* made of this silk in a pattern of small squares of different shades of blue.

From Amarapura they proceeded to the Mahagandaryone Monastery. Although King Mindon's desire to make Mandalay a centre for Buddhist teaching did not succeed, his legacy has left the city with many fine monasteries, and the Mahagandaryone Monastery is one of them. The Monastery is a complex of buildings consisting of living quarters, communal baths and kitchen, prayer halls and a large dining room. It was obviously popular and well off, because he noticed a number of new, substantial, buildings near the entrance. As is well known, Buddhist monks visit designated households each morning to receive either rice or a curry of some sort. They then bring the food back to their monastery where it is consumed before mid-day. That is their one meal for the day. Soon after they arrived, the monks and rather young novices were beginning to congregate and form themselves into different queues. At the stroke of a gong they all trooped into the dining hall in an orderly fashion and took their allotted places on mats in front of long low tables and began their meal. They ate with concentration and dignity, but in silence.

Talking to his guide, he remembered how it was customary for all young boys to enter the Monkhood for varying lengths of time, at least once in their lives. He then recalled how the older of the two brothers who were his neighbours in the house on stilts many years ago, entered the Monkhood. An elderly monk came one morning, and in his presence the boy's head was shaved. He then had a bath and put on the saffron coloured robe of the Monkhood before *shiko*-ing before the older monk, asking to be taken into the order. Upon acceptance by the older monk, the boy left with him for the monastery. The next day and for the rest of the week he came back to his house in the mornings to collect food, and his parents had to *shiko* before him, because he was now not their son, but a member of the *Sangha* or Monkhood.

The length of time that a young boy spends at the Monastery varies considerably. Some stay for just a day, most usually stay for at least a week, whilst some decide that they want to give up the secular world and become a monk.

From the Mahagandaryone Monastery they proceeded to the starting point of the U Bain Bridge, a wooden bridge 1.2km in length built about 200 years ago. The bridge actually spans a tributary of the Irrawaddy river, and when crossing it, he noticed that many men and women were involved in fishing near the bridge, walking chest deep in the water, which could not have been very deep at that point. On the bridge itself, numerous craftsmen (he would not call them artists, although they produced pictures) were using charcoal or ink and rapidly producing small vignettes of stereotyped native scenes. He also noticed a number of young people, some pushing bicycles, coming in the opposite direction carrying books, and learnt that there was a university on the other side of the bridge. Immediately upon alighting from the bridge, he found himself in a kind of village square. Unpaved and surrounded on all sides by one-storeyed thatch houses that served for the most part as studios, the square was not without charm, for in-between the houses, banana plants grew regal and bedraggled, showing off their yellow and sepulchral hues. Unfortunately, the watercolours on display were rather stiff, and lacking in originality. Nonetheless, they did reveal the artistic bent of the people, although he could not help but wonder whether there was a market was for all the works produced.

Rather than retrace their steps on the bridge they decided to take a long rowing boat back. On the way, they passed other boats whose passengers hid under umbrellas as the sun was becoming increasingly hot. Unfortunately, their boat managed to get entangled with some fishing nets, and in the resultant delay it soon became stifling, so he was glad to get back to the car. It was then time for lunch at a Chinese restaurant housed in an old mansion with a garden in front. At the hotel, he was rather surprised to see his name on the notice board welcoming visitors. The hotel room itself was spacious, well-appointed and over looked Mandalay Hill, but the management was rather mean as there were no coffee or tea making facilities. However, he did not have time to brood over this, because it was soon time to set off on the visit to Mandalay Palace.

King Mindon's palace was unfortunately badly damaged during the Second World War, and apart from the old city wall and the moat, has been largely rebuilt. It is an attractive edifice nonetheless, and looking at the exhibition of King Mindon and his reign, he recalled how ill prepared the last King of the country, King Thibaw, was to meet the challenge of the British flotilla. This was partly because of the lies that he was told by his advisers who kept on telling him the British had been defeated and would never arrive at Mandalay. Then, like now, in an Eastern setting, no one wished to be the harbinger of bad news, lest the wrath of the hearer fell on them. The war which ceded the whole of the country to the British was, like most wars of the nineteenth century, really about trading rights and, in this case, the dispute centred on the supply of teak wood, although French ambitions also had a part to play. Upon King Thibaw's defeat, the British arranged to send him, his Queen Supayalat, who some say was the real power behind the throne and a ruthless one at that, and his daughters into exile in India without delay, lest their presence in Mandalay became the rallying point for uprisings in the country. So ended a reign that began in a bloody fashion when any one who had the slightest claim to the throne was assassinated or put to death.

Today the complex in which the palace is situated is a security area housing the military. Upon leaving the complex, he noticed a large sign, which said something like 'The Thatmadaw would never betray the National Interest'. He asked the guide what 'Thatmadaw' meant, and was told it was the name for military. Well, they may or may not betray the national interest, but they have certainly taken over all the prestigious areas and buildings, and are now the new Royalty of the country.

Chapter Eight ~
Largest Book in the World

The visit to the temples housing Buddha images of various ages and in different materials was interesting, but not nearly as interesting as the adjacent library which was specially opened for him, and which houses thousand of scholarly works written on palm leaves. Most of the works were of a religious nature and probably rarely consulted, but he could still not help but wonder how much longer they would be preserved in a non air-conditioned environment. But being on palm leaves, maybe air-conditioning would not really suit them.

In contrast, there were no such worries for the 'largest book in the world'. Actually, the billing is a bit misleading, because it was not a book in the conventional sense, but marble tablets inscribed with the *Tipitaka* or Buddhist scriptures. Each tablet was housed in its own individual stupa, and there were dozens of stupas, all in dazzling white.

He then proceeded to the Shweinpin Monastery, made entirely of teak wood, and decorated with exquisite carvings, before ascending Mandalay Hill for a panoramic view of the city, which seemed rather flat and agrarian. However, the guide proudly pointed out the golf course, as well as his own resort hotel at the foot of the hill.

Breakfast the next morning, which was of the usual buffet type, known sometimes as 'American breakfast', was interesting in revealing the mix of people staying at the hotel. There were the usual ageing continental Europeans, some of whom didn't speak any English, as well as a particularly noisy group who spoke volubly and were rather uncouth, piling their plates with food, determined to get their money's worth. It was little wonder, then, that most of them were of considerable girth. He could not make out whether they were from northern Thailand or from Yunnan in China.

Watching his intake of cholesterol, there wasn't a great deal that was suitable for him to eat, and he was disappointed that the buffet table didn't feature any traditional dishes of the country. Why, he wondered, did the country not promote its own cuisine, which was as good as anything produced in neighbouring Thailand. It is hardly surprising then that there are few restaurants overseas offering the country's food, whereas Thai restaurants can be found in abundance. Reflecting on this he downed two excellent hot cups of coffee and was ready for the day's excursion.

It was, in fact, a rather leisurely day. The first stop was to a local grocer, as he wanted to buy some sweets for the children that he was likely to meet during the day. The day before some of them had asked for bon-bon and he didn't understand until the guide told him that the word stood for sweets. At the grocery shop he also bought sweets for the guide's daughter who was eleven years old, as well as for the driver's children.

Looking for a local jacket as well as dress slippers to go with his silk *longyi*, he was taken by the guide to the well-known market. At the market he noticed a number of *tongas* which he loved to ride in his childhood, as well as bullock carts heavily laden with bags of rice and other produce. At the market he bought a nice pair of rubber-soled, velvet-topped slippers for the equivalent of one United States dollar. Unfortunately, he couldn't get a jacket in the right size and colour, but he did get a small but good Burmese phrase book, and encouraged his guide to produce a recording to go with the book.

It was then on to the Mahamuni temple, which is probably the most sacred shrine in the city. Legend has it that the Buddha statue was cast during the life time of Gautama, the fourth Buddha, but it probably dates from the first century. Cast in bronze, it has accumulated so much gold that it now looks a bit lopsided. Only men are allowed to apply the gold foil to the statue, which seemed a bit strange considering that images of the Buddha could take both a male and female form and the same rule did not apply at the Shwedagon in the capital.

He felt very fortunate to witness an initiation procession for the Shin-pyu ceremony, involving a number of young boys who were to be initiated into the Monkhood. He had read that in olden times these processions could be quite spectacular. That which he witnessed was a more modest affair. Nevertheless, the boys and older relatives were dressed in traditional finery, and some carried the large stupa-like umbrellas typical of the country. They did not mind in the least having their photograph taken. It was then time for lunch, and he was delighted when the guide told him that he was to have a native meal. They duly made their way to the restaurant, getting a table near the large glass windows overlooking the street, and had a very good meal of a variety of dishes. All were referred to as curry, but many of the dishes were not really curries in the accepted sense, but the vocabulary in English for the dishes is limited, so it was easier for the guide simply to refer to the dishes as curries. Each dish seemed to take on the colour of its main ingredients, and some were green, others red and some darkish brown. It was the best meal of native cuisine he had in the country.

It was then a short drive to the river bank for the boat ride to Mingun across the Irrawaddy river. In order to get to their boat, they had to climb over five other boats, and this sort of thing always made him nervous, as his eyesight is not what it used to be. The boat ride was calm and leisurely, and with the cool breezes gently caressing him, he never felt more at peace. Despite this, he could not help but notice the make-shift thatch shacks of the fishermen on the river banks, and knew that it must be a hard life for them. He also saw a few buffaloes wallowing in the river bed. Approaching

Mingun he noticed from a distance a reddish squat structure, which he later was to learn was the massive but uncompleted Mantara Gyi pagoda, built by forced labour. The slaves came from Arakan on the western side of the country, and the enforced labour prompted a guerilla war against the king which eventually erupted into the First Anglo-Burmese war.

The nearby Mingun bell, the second largest of its kind in the world, and the world's largest ringing bell, made a glorious deep reverberating sound when struck with a wooden hammer. They then walked through the village, and he thought to himself that it was obviously well organized for tourism with numerous shops selling souvenirs and not very good water colours of native scenery. However, he was delighted to see part of the lifestyle of the village, including a home for the aged, where the elderly people were obviously happy. As is usual with villages in the country, there were no paved roads and the paths and alleyways were of beaten red earth. During the Monsoon season he could just visualize them turning muddy with rivulets of water, making them impassable to those with shoes.

Dinner at a well-known Chinese restaurant in the city wasn't very good, and the restaurant's specialty, roast duck, was inedible. However, the guide was happy to have it packed to take home. Back at the hotel it was time to say good-bye to his well-educated guide, who had excused himself from seeing him off at the airport the next morning, as his younger brother was getting married.

Talking to his guide, he learnt that his brother and his wife-to-be would be living together with the guide and his family and the guide's mother in 'one compound', as the guide put it. He could not help reflecting that unlike individualistic Western families, Eastern families continue to stick together even after marriage. Whilst this can cause tensions and inevitably means a certain loss of freedom and privacy, it can also be a tower of strength during times of crisis and ill health. According to the guide, marriages did not have to take place in a temple or civil marriage registry, but usually took place at home in the presence of family and friends. For his brother's wedding, the groom had invited a few monks home to witness and bless the ceremony, and that was it. Despite the apparent casualness or simplicity of the marriage ceremony, marriages in the country tend to be long lasting, and, certainly, women enjoy a freedom undreamt of in many Asian countries. On marriage, they retain their own names. They have equal rights of inheritance with men, and are accepted as equal partners in all business endeavours. Indeed, they are usually the brains behind their husbands' successes.

To those brought up in a Westernized tradition, the arrangements may seen rather casual, but then there is a disdain for the niceties of legality or bureaucracy in the country, and he recalled how his own birth certificate simply stated 'a son to Mr & Mrs' without any proper names. Later in life, he had a devilish time proving that he was indeed the son of that particular Mr & Mrs. It was a surreal experience, knowing who you are and not being able to prove it.

Chapter Nine ~ The Shan States

It was another early morning start, but this time, mercifully, with breakfast first, as the hotel started restaurant service at five thirty in the morning.

Helio airport in the Shan States, despite being a small one storeyed building, was tight on security, and upon entering the small arrival hall, two young women took charge of his luggage tag and passport. He then had to walk out of the building on a gravel path to a gate, and it was only outside the gate that his guide met him. Unlike his other guides, his guide this time was of considerable height and girth, typical of inhabitants of the Shan States, but with a friendly demeanour. He learnt later that the airport was strong on security because Helio was close to the drug trafficking center.

To get to his hotel on Inle lake, it was initially a long drive over a winding road, which was first built by the British about sixty years ago and was now being repaired. On arrival at the lake, they visited a local market whose stalls offered a mixture of food, local produce, including native peanut sweets, and household goods. At the market he noticed a number of Paungdung women wearing head scarves or turbans, as the guide called them, but saw none of the long-necked women with brass rings around their necks. They then embarked on a long narrow motorized boat, and it was another half an hour before they reached the landing of the hotel. Enroute he noticed a hive of activity at many of the houses on stilts which banked onto the lake. Some people were doing their morning ablutions, and others were washing clothes or cooking pots and pans. There were also small groups huddled around small coal fires.

The hotel was of the resort type, but made entirely of wood and thatched bamboo. However, service was of a high standard. He was escorted to his bungalow, and the hotel's facilities were explained to him. He was, of course, familiar with room service and the usual menu for it, but was a bit surprised to hear the girl point to a 'menu' for hotel services and a 'menu' for spa treatments. Computer-speak seemed to have permeated everywhere. Prices were comparable to international rates, and were more expensive than at the hotel in the capital. Also despite the wood and thatch make up and the mosquito net hanging over the bed, the bungalow was equipped with all 'mod cons'. After choosing his meal for dinner, which was included in the room rate, it was time to set-off on his day's excursion around the lake.

They had a lot of ground to cover, because Inle lake is about 15 miles in length. But the boat was swift and the ride was really delightful. His first sight was of a lone fisherman, rowing his boat with one leg, whilst small flocks of gulls or egrets flitted here and there. They passed a clutter of houses, and he noticed a sign which said 'Ann's: fine French food', so the lake inhabitants were not lacking in sophistication.

Their first stop was the Phaungdaw Oo Pagoda, which is famous for its five Buddha images. Like many such images, they were originally cast much smaller, but had been built up over the years by the accumulation of gold leaf applied by devotees. Each year rather like the statues in a Roman Catholic church, these Buddha images are taken out in a boat procession. One year, the boat carrying the images collapsed. Devotees managed to salvage only four of the images, but failed to find the fifth image despite repeated efforts. Imagine their surprise when on returning to the Pagoda rather crestfallen they found the fifth image on its usual place on the altar.

On leaving the pagoda, children came around for their usual bon-bons and he was somewhat surprised that even grown women asked for some. As usual, the children wore Western-style clothing, but the clothes were an odd mixture of mis-matched items and were obviously 'hand-me downs' from some charitable organization.

From the pagoda they proceeded to lunch at a two-storeyed wooden restaurant where they got a table on the balcony of the upper floor, so he had a good view of the hamlet as well as activity on the lake. Children from the hamlet went to school by walking over a number of wooden bridges. Lunch was passable, and he noticed an enormous avocado, which the locals ate either with lemon juice squeezed over the fruit, or with condensed milk for a different taste.

It was then on to the Ngaplechaung Monastery, which was well-known for its youthful Buddha images, as well as its jumping cats. The Buddhas had sweet expressions on their faces, and the cats, which had been taught by the monks to jump through a small bamboo loop, were interesting for a while. Enroute to the Monastery they passed the floating gardens, but they were not particularly interesting. Maybe it was the wrong time of the year, and the flowers were not in bloom.

The silver and textile cottage industries which he visited were the usual mixture of a few workers and a shop at the end. He always found visits to these so-called workshops disappointing because there is little to be seen of the various processes that go into the make-up of the final product, and this occasion was no exception. However, both the silver work and silks were of a fine quality, if expensive by the standards of the country. At the textiles industry a group of women weavers were taking a rest and offered to share their peanuts with him. At the shop he looked in vain for the royal blue cloth which he had seen on the loom. Although they offered to cut a piece for him, the price quoted was too high, so he concentrated on the scarves and managed to get two really nice silk ones.

On returning to the hotel he decided to have a drink on the restaurant's balcony to watch the sun set, which was a mistake. The cocktail was the usual sweet concoction, which he did not enjoy, and the balcony soon became very cold to sit on. However, a nice hot bath soon revived him, and he was ready for his dinner. His pre-ordered meal came on an enormous platter, rather like an Indian thali, and was quite tasty. However, the bottle of Australian red wine that he decided to splurge on was disappointing, being both alcoholic and tannic. It was then to his room where he noticed that the mosquito net had been let down, his bed made ready for sleeping and a hot water bottle placed between the blankets. He tried to read, but was soon asleep.

He woke at five thirty to a freezing cold morning, so he hurriedly dressed and proceeded, still under darkness, to the restaurant building for breakfast, and was the first customer there. The breakfast was good and warming, and it was soon time to retrace his steps. His guide was waiting for him by the boat landing and suggested that he sit at the rear of the boat. However, noticing the day before that the rear of the boat tended to attract spray from the boat's engine, he opted to sit in front. This soon proved to be a mistake, because when the boat picked up speed it became increasingly cold and he was soon chilled to the bone, despite seeking protection from his wool scarf and an umbrella. Despite the cold, the white low mist all around the boat and the layer upon layer of undulating blue hills in the distance was a magnificent sight.

On land once again, he discussed with his large Shan guide the previous independence of the Shan States under British rule, as well as the well-known British administrator, Sir George Scott, who is still remembered even to-day in the Shan States, but under his Burmese name. Back home, he tried to look for Scott's famous book 'The Burman' on the internet but had no luck. He then remembered that Scott had a Burmese name, so searched under Shwe Yoe, and managed to trace the book, which has been reprinted by a Scottish firm. He is now the proud owner of a copy of this book, which is a mine of information.

Chapter Ten~Yangon Again

The flight back to Yangon was uneventful, but on arrival in the capital the wait for his baggage was almost as long as the flight. His guide was happy to see him, and it was straight back to his hotel in the centre of the city. He noticed, that, having complained about the van provided before, his guide had arranged for a saloon car with a new driver, who was a handsome young man and looked very Eurasian.

After checking in it was time for lunch. He felt like having a good *Mohinga* before leaving the country, so checked the room service menu and found that it was listed. He thought to himself, if room service has the dish, then the coffee shop should also have it. However, before taking his seat he asked the waitress if they served Mohinga. She said, rather in surprise, "Traditional Mohinga?" then checked the menu to confirm that they did indeed serve it. It was the best Mohinga he had had for a long time. The fish broth was thick and plentiful, also piquant as he remembered it and the white rice noodles came with all the condiments on the side.

With the aid of the driver and guide and his city map, he then went in search of the school that he had attended for about a year and a half. It was exactly as he remembered it, the low red brick buildings set in the form of a U-shape with the playing field in front of the central building that served as the morning assembly hall. From the depths of his memory, he could hear the steps of the school principal as he made his way to morning assembly. As the steps grew louder and closer a hush used to fall over the assembled boys. The principal was probably a kindly man, but a stern one, and all of the boys were rather in awe of him. A large signboard in Burmese gave the current name of the school, but he was delighted to discover on the old brick gate posts the old name of his school: 'St. John's Diocesan Boys' School'. He wanted to go into the school to see the old assembly hall, and his old class room, but a rather officious lady said in a kind of high giggly voice "Sorry, we need the permission of the education ministry before we can allow you in".

Then they drove past the Women's Hospital (was it called the Dufferin Hospital before where he was in fact born?) and past the small local railway station just below a small bridge. All this was as he remembered it. However, from then on, the road no longer looked the same, so it came as quite a surprise when he suddenly noticed on the left hand side of the road, the large building where his piano teacher used to live. She occupied a small flat on the ground floor at the rear of the building, and he remembered that after just a few lessons he was playing scales quite competently. It was obviously the flexibility of his young hands at work. Regrettably, the weekly piano lessons came to an abrupt halt about two months later because his father could not afford to pay the tuition fees and also considered that piano lessons were not really of much use.

It was then a quick right turn, and sooner than expected, the old British Council's official residence came into view. He had lived there for a while, and had never been happier. He was amazed that it was still there, but it now looked rather neglected and forlorn. The house itself obviously needed a good coat of paint, whilst the garden needed attending to. For some reason he did not venture further than the open gate, although the guide was keen to go into the garden with him. However, the memories came flooding back. He remembered how his godfather who was then head of the British Council in the country used to keep a devoted south Indian butler named Swami. The butler, who lived with his family in the rear of the compound, was all gold teeth and smiles, but he was efficient. He not only drew a bath, but also laid out his godfather's clothes each day, deciding what was appropriate. During meal times at the tinkle of a bell he used to bring in each course of their meal, which they used to take in his godfather's private sitting room. He recalled how his godfather took him to see a film at a private club on the royal lakes. On their return, they found that the butler had arranged for hot cocoa in a flask and a marmite sandwich to be placed at their respective bedsides. A marmite sandwich never tasted better to his young hungry appetite. The British Council residence used to retain a gurkha night watchman. During examination time, he asked the watchman to wake

69

him at 4:00 AM by tapping on the outside of his room, so that he could get up to study. Unfortunately, the tapping only served to wake his godfather in the adjacent room, who was rather annoyed, so the tapping had to stop. On one occasion, his godfather had to travel up-country, and asked him what he wanted to do about his meals. He decided to take a cash allowance, and on the first day asked the cook to roast him a chicken. The intention was he would eat the chicken over several days and thus pocket some of the food allowance. Unfortunately, when the roast chicken was done he kept on nibbling at it periodically and then found to his horror that he had eaten the whole chicken in less than one day.

The guide said to him, "Uncle, what was the road called before?" In answer he said "Windsor Road". "Oh", said the guide, "That is why the hotel down the road is called Windsor Hotel". And sure enough, a few houses down, the 'Windsor Hotel' came into view. Strange, he thought, how governments might wish to erase the past and rename roads, yet, the people needed roots and still cherish the past.

It now remained to do a bit of last minute shopping, although he still did not have luck in getting a traditional Burmese jacket despite visiting two markets and a special tailor shop. In his wanderings he could not but fail to notice that the old trishaws were no longer in existence. Unlike trishaws elsewhere, these were built rather like the old motorcycles with sidecars. When he was young they were a relatively nice, if expensive, way to get around the city. He also could not find the Burmese candy made with tropical fruit, but as he was getting tired, the guide suggested that he would look for the sweets.

True to his promise the guide did indeed find the sweets and gave them to him when he picked him up from the hotel in the evening. Knowing that he had had Mohinga for lunch and a preference for native cuisine, the guide arranged to take him to a neighbourhood restaurant for dinner. The waitresses were friendly and helpful and were delighted to have their photographs taken. Some of the food was good, particularly the 'Pennyworth salad', but all through his journey he was wary of salads and cut fruits as well as un-bottled water, so only ate a bit of the salad. After dinner, the guide suggested that they go to a neighbourhood café for coffee. There was little to distinguish the café from similar cafes elsewhere, but once again the staff were friendly, and it was good to be able to see how the locals lived and to soak up the dimly lit surroundings.

The attempt to visit the externally brightly lit Chinese temple proved futile as it was closed. The driver then suggested that they visit the temple on the outskirts of the city, but that too proved unsuccessful. He then had a last look at the city by night before returning to his hotel.

It was yet another early morning start, and after a quick breakfast at the coffee shop, he was on his way to the airport by six in the morning. Enroute he noticed a number of morning walkers, as well as a small group doing exercise. It was still dark at this time and he had a last look at the shimmering golden Shwedagon in the distance and felt a wrench in his heart. However he soon arrived at the airport and it was time to say 'goodbye' to his guide and driver. The guide said, "Uncle, you must come back again soon".

At the airport, the Myanmar Airways staff appeared to be half asleep, from the check-in staff to the air crew. The chief steward was not only unable to provide the dish he wanted for lunch, but also managed to spill tomato juice all over him, and then made matters worse by trying to rub it off with a fluffy paper towel. However, by this time, some of the serenity of the country had rubbed off on him, so he took these minor mishaps in his stride.

Conclusion~The Golden Land

If any reader has persevered so far, they will have noticed that this account is more than that of a visit to a relatively unknown country. It is also in part a personal journey through time, and in part a scattered history of a country that has still to realize its full potential.

On completion of his journey, he looked at his passport and noted for the first time a condition to his visa. 'Land Use Not Permissible' it said. Although the cynic would say that the condition had been imposed lest he see too much, he likes to think that it was there for his own protection.

It was an exciting yet emotional visit for him, and he will, in time, definitely go back to this shining, smiling, golden land, that is the country of his birth.